Nancy Prince

Dedicated
to
The Friends of Wilson Lake
and the Loons of Wilson Lake

Special thanks to Chelsea Seabold,
who modeled for the book.

Libby's Loons
Copyright © 2010 by Nancy Prince
Illustrations copyright © by Luanne Wrenn

ISBN: 978-1-934582-27-5

BACK CHANNEL PRESS
170 Mechanic Street
Portsmouth, NH 03801
www.backchannelpress.com
Printed in the United States of America

Layout by John & Nancy Grossman

Library of Congress PCN 2010911452

Libby's Loons

by
Nancy Prince

Illustrated by Luanne Wrenn

www.nancyprinceofmaine.com

back channel press
portsmouth, new hampshire

"They're back!" Libby sat up in her bed.
"I hear them," she whispered, as
laughing calls floated across the lake and
drifted through her bedroom window.
"The loons are back!"

Spring had come to the lake. Melting ice brought the return of rippling water and the arrival of wildlife to its shores. Libby could watch turtles sunning on logs...

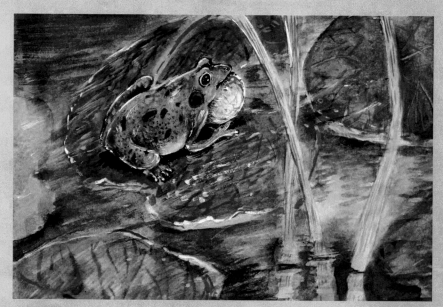

...bullfrogs on lily pads croaking,

"Chug-er-um..."

...and ducklings following their mothers,
"Quack, quack, quack."

Libby's favorite inhabitants of the lake were the loons. Ice-out always signaled their return to the lake.

Libby loved to paddle her kayak into the marsh to look for loons. Each year a pair of the large, black and white birds nested in the sweet smelling marsh grass near her home.

Every spring Libby waited eagerly to see
if there would be a loon baby or two.
This year she was not disappointed.

On her first paddle of the season she spotted two adult loons. The smaller female loon had a fuzzy brown bump on her back.

"A new loon chick!" exclaimed Libby as she drew close. "I'll name you Chicklet."

Libby watched for the chick every day. When it grew too big to ride on the parents' backs, the baby usually swam snugly between the two adults.

Please keep Chicklet safe from snapping turtles and eagles, wished Libby.

Libby learned to recognize the loons' fierce cries when eagles or airplanes flew overhead. Those loud screams were not at all like the sounds of their enchanting wails and yodels.

Sometimes Libby noticed the loon parents warning away boaters. With wings spread wide, they raised their bodies as if standing on water. They made themselves look threatening to protect their family.

Libby called it their "Penguin Dance."

On a warm, summer day butterflies circled Libby's kayak. A dragonfly took a ride on her paddle.

Libby was surprised when the male loon appeared close by, calling a soft "hoot." Then she saw the female and chick in a nearby cove.

Oh, he's not talking to me, she thought. *He's calling his family*.

She stopped paddling, letting the kayak float on the still water.

As each adult upended and slid beneath the water, the baby would duck its head under the surface. Libby wished she could see what Chicklet was seeing. When the father emerged with a fish the little loon propelled itself toward him. It snatched the wiggling morsel.

Libby's nose wrinkled. "Eeuwe," she muttered, "I'm glad I don't have to eat what Chicklet is eating!"

After that day the loons allowed Libby to
come close enough to watch the young one's
diving and fishing lessons. She was always
careful to remain respectfully outside the
family group. One time Chicklet swam up to
her kayak, but a gentle "hoot" brought it back
to its parent's side.

In late summer, flight school began. Chicklet looked like a whirly-bird lawn ornament to Libby as it flapped its little wings along the waves.

By early fall the young loon had almost mastered flight, but Libby was worried. Would Chicklet be able to fly before winter?

The loons must leave the lake before the ice formed. She knew that loons need lots of space to get off the water because of their heavy bodies.

One September afternoon, Libby paddled toward the mouth of the cove to watch take-off practice.

As she glanced up at the sky an eagle appeared, its wings widespread, white head looking low. It spied the whirling wings of the little loon.

The eagle swooped. He dropped suddenly, crashing onto the water. Splash!

Chicklet tumbled out of sight. The mother loon screamed. Libby screamed. The mother raced to the rescue.

Libby paddled furiously toward the eagle. "No! No!" she shouted.

The eagle gave up the attack, abandoning the lake to perch on the barren branch of a pine tree.

Mother loon, with the chick safely by her side, rose up on the water. She lifted her outstretched wings in warning.

Libby, too, scolded the eagle as it stared down from the branch above her head. "Naughty bird! Go away! Eat your fish and leave my loon alone!"

As if her words were heard, the majestic bird spread its wings and soared away.

In October, the weather changed. Autumn's red and gold leaves began to blur into brown as they drifted down onto the cove. A cold wind blew across the lake.

It was time to store the kayak for the winter. Libby could still view the loon family from the shore. She watched the black and white pattern of the adults' feathers gradually fade as they molted to their winter colors of grey, brown and white.

Ice began to form along the shoreline of the lake. Libby was afraid that Chicklet might not learn to fly in time to join the yearly trip to the open water of the ocean.

Then one late fall day she heard a commotion above the lake.

Libby peered up into the sky to see three young loons in flight. They called to Chicklet as the frantic young loon splashed along the water, desperately trying to join them.

Libby held her breath. "C'mon, Chicklet, I know you can do it."

All at once Chicklet gave a swish of its wings, rose up off the lake and soared into the blue sky. "You've done it!" she shouted.

"Good luck! Safe journey."

Did you know that ...?

Loons are migratory birds that breed on lakes and spend winters on the ocean.

Loons make four different calls, the wail, yodel, tremolo, and hoot.

Through observations of banded male loons, it appears that the yodel call may be used to indicate territory; individual males may alter or mimic yodel calls when changing territory.

Adult loons molt, or lose and grow new feathers, twice a year. In the winter they are mostly gray and in the summer they are black with speckles of white.

Both the male and female take turns incubating the eggs and share in all the parenting responsibilities.

Young chicks ride on their parent's backs when chilled. This also protects them from predators.

Loons reach two years of age before they acquire their black and white breeding plumage, and during that time, they stay on the ocean.

The oldest known loon is 20 years (and counting). Researchers have learned this through bird banding.

Improperly disposed fishing line and lead tackle are serious threats to loons.

These loon facts have been provided by Patrick Keenan, Outreach Coordinator for BioDiversity Research Institute (BRI), a science-based nonprofit located in Gorham, ME. To learn more about BRI visit www.briloon.org.

Wilton, Maine school children participate annually in an educational program on loons and loon research offered by BioDiversity Research Institute. The project is facilitated by Nancy Prince under the sponsorship of Friends of Wilson Lake.